JAMES MARSHALL · SWINE

MICHAEL DI CAPUA BOOKS

LAKE · MAURICE SENDAK

HARPER COLLINS PUBLISHERS

One wintry afternoon a lean and mangy wolf found himself in an unfamiliar part of town.

"I don't know where I am," he said, "but it's important to explore new places and expand one's horizons. I might discover all *sorts* of tasty morsels."

Two young squirrels rounded the corner and scampered past.

"Look at that poor old dog," one of them said. "He's on his last legs." And the squirrels were gone.

"Humph!" snorted the wolf. "Lucky for them I'm not so swift as I used to be. Squirrel makes a superb afternoon snack." Winding his ratty scarf around his neck, he continued on down the street.

"Old dog, indeed!" he muttered. In the middle of the next block, the wolf's nose began to twitch uncontrollably. A delicious aroma permeated the air.

"Well, I declare!" he cried. "I think I smell . . . Oh, my goodness, could it be? . . . Yes, that's it all right! I'd recognize that smell anywhere!" He looked up and down the street, but there were no pigs about.

"I don't see them," said the wolf, "but they're somewhere in the vicinity, that's for sure."

A theater marquee on the opposite side of the street attracted his attention.

"Do my eyes deceive me?" gasped the wolf. "Does that say what I think it says?" Stepping across the street, he looked up at the marquee, which spelled out in large letters:

Many photographs of the production were displayed outside the theater. Really, it was unbelievable! There were pigs in every picture. Leaping, swirling, bowing, juicy pigs. The wolf's heart was racing, his paws were trembling.

"Scrumptious! Scrumptious!" he exclaimed, dabbing drops of saliva from his lips.

As he studied the photographs, the wolf was oblivious to his surroundings. Suddenly he realized that a large crowd had gathered on the sidewalk. Sleek limousines were gliding up to the curb, and well-dressed hogs were emerging and making their way into the theater. The wolf pulled up his collar and tried to make himself as inconspicuous as possible.

Soon the aroma of pig, thinly disguised by French perfume, was making him swoon. Losing all self-restraint, he decided to waste no more time and pounce on the nearest pig. But several police officers were milling about.

"Not a good idea," he said to himself. "Besides, what I really want is *inside* the theater."

He observed that everyone entering the theater presented a ticket at the door.

"I'll have to purchase one," he said. But when he looked into his coin purse, he saw that he was completely without funds.

"They'll never let me in without a ticket!" he cried in despair.

At that moment a limousine rolled up in front of the theater and a fat old sow squeezed herself out onto the sidewalk. Squinting through her lorgnette, she said to the wolf, "Did you need a pair of tickets? My husband and I are tied up this evening and are unable to attend. He hates the ballet, you know,

and will find *any* excuse. They're excellent seats. Very near the stage."

The wolf, who couldn't believe his luck, snatched the tickets from the old sow and pushed his way into the crowd. "Well, I never!" said the sow, climbing back into her limousine.

At the theater door, the wolf presented his ticket and stepped inside. (Had the ticket taker been more observant, he would have noticed the long claws and much that follows could have been avoided.)

Once inside—and he had never been in a real theater before—the wolf looked around with considerable interest. Everywhere he turned, pigs and hogs were standing about and chatting excitedly. Although some of them were wearing perfectly outlandish clothes, the others seemed not to take the slightest notice. The wolf moved easily through the crowd.

"They'll notice me soon enough," he thought.

An usher, dreamily lost in a book, escorted him to his seat.

"Best seats in the house," she said. "You have a box all to yourself."

The wolf slipped into his seat and was decidedly pleased.

"It's only a short leap onto the stage," he said.

As the orchestra in the pit was tuning up, his stomach grumbled in anticipation.

"I must remember not to gobble my food," he said.

Soon the theater was filled to capacity. As the lights began to dim, a hush fell over the audience. It was a magical moment, and the wolf held his breath.

A burst of applause greeted the conductor as he made his way through the orchestra. Mounting the podium, he bowed to the audience and beamed into the spotlight. The applause swelled. The conductor turned, nodded to his musicians, and lowered his baton. The music began, and the curtain rose on an empty stage flooded with light.

"Where are the pigs?" said the wolf.

At that moment, from each side of the stage, dancing pigs appeared. They were wearing brightly colored costumes and were extremely happy about something. The wolf's mouth dropped open. The pigs were even plumper and juicier than he'd imagined.

"Photographs don't do them justice!" he gasped.

He began to consider his selection. Of course, he would eat them *all*, but why not have the juiciest first? He leaned forward to get a better look at the entrancing spectacle. But as his eyes darted from one dancer to another, he noticed that some sort of story was being told. "What's going on?" he said. "Someone seems to be getting married."

On the stage the pigs were dancing about on their toes and tossing rose petals in the air. The wedding couple made an entrance and did a little dance, which was well received by the audience.

The mangy wolf, who couldn't wait a moment longer, decided to take action. He rose from his seat.

Suddenly, from the back of the stage, a ferocious monster appeared and scattered the terrified wedding party in all directions. Executing some thrilling leaps, the monster snatched the pig bride and carried her off. The bridegroom fainted, and the curtain came down to tremendous applause.

"Gosh!" said the wolf.

He remained in his seat during intermission and studied his program. "I'll make my big move in Act Two," he said.

After a quarter of an hour, the lights in the theater blinked off and on, and the audience hurried back to their seats. Act Two had always been a big favorite.

Act Two, Scene One took place in the monster's cave. When the curtain rose, the monster was seen busily preparing a boiling kettle in which to cook the unhappy pig.

"This is thrilling!" said the wolf, who was closely following the action on stage.

Just as the monster was about to toss the pig into the kettle, an old crone appeared at the door of the cave and danced in. She offered the monster a nectarine, and no sooner had the monster nibbled on the nectarine than he fell asleep.

Suddenly the old crone threw off her cape and mask—it was the handsome bridegroom come to rescue his bride. The two pigs did a dance of joy and hurried out of the cave.

Act Two, Scene Two took place on the banks of Swine Lake.

It was clear from the exciting music that the monster was in hot pursuit of the pig couple and that he was fast approaching. The pigs, unable to swim, prepared to meet their fate and did a sad little dance.

At this moment, from out of the lake, the Enchanted Pig appeared, gathered them up in her velvet wings, and carried them across to safety.

When the curtain fell, there were many shouts of "Bravo!"

The dancers took many well-deserved bows, and the show was over. The wolf staggered out of the theater in a trance. He had completely forgotten to make his move. He wasn't even hungry anymore.

"Been up to no good, I imagine," grumbled his landlady on the stairs. The mangy wolf did not seem to hear, went up to his bare attic room, crawled into bed, and took a long nap. He dreamed of dancing pigs.

That night he did something he'd never done before—he broke into his piggy bank. Then he tore down the stairs and ran all the way to the theater, where he spent his last penny on an excellent seat for the evening performance of *Swine Lake*.

When the curtain went up, the mangy wolf found himself absorbed in the story all over again. The bride and groom made their entrance and did their little dance.

"Now comes the good part with the monster," said the wolf.

The music soared. Suddenly, without knowing why, the wolf sprang out of his seat, leapt over the railing, sailed right over the orchestra pit and onto the stage. The audience gasped, and the orchestra kept right on playing.

Carried away with the music, the wolf began to swirl about
the stage. The pig dancing the part of the bride was confused.

"Who are you?" she said in a stage whisper.

"Just keep dancing!" the wolf whispered back.

The audience, too, was somewhat confused. "They've changed the steps," someone complained.

At the proper moment, the wolf picked up the frightened

bride and carried her offstage. The bridegroom fainted, and the curtain fell. The applause was tremendous.

"Such an interesting interpretation!" someone said.

Dropping the pig ballerina backstage, the wolf ran past the startled stage manager, out the stage door, and down the street. He did not stop running until he reached home.

"Quite out of breath, eh?" said his landlady. "Leading a life of crime, no doubt."

"You wouldn't understand," said the wolf.

The next day, in a newspaper he found on a park bench, the mangy wolf read a review of *Swine Lake*.

The wolf tore out the review and shoved it in his pocket.
"A real wolf, indeed!" he said. And he executed a couple of
flashy dance steps.